For Ineke, and all who miss her

First published in Great Britain in 2010 by Andersen Press Ltd.,
20 Vauxhall Bridge Road, London SW1V 2SA.
Published in Australia by Random House Australia Pty.,
Level 3, 100 Pacific Highway, North Sydney, NSW 2060.
Copyright © Paul Geraghty, 2010
The rights of Paul Geraghty to be identified as the
author and illustrator of this work have been asserted by him in
accordance with the Copyright, Designs and Patents Act, 1988.
All rights reserved.
Colour separated in Switzerland by Photolitho AG, Zürich.
Printed and bound in Singapore by Tien Wah Press.
Paul Geraghty has used watercolour in this book.

10 9 8 7 6 5 4 3 2 1

British Library Cataloguing in Publication Data available.

ISBN 978 1 84270 979 5 (hardback) ISBN 978 1 84939 027 9 (paperback)

This book has been printed on acid-free paper

HELP ME!

PAUL GERAGHTY

ANDERSEN PRESS

Beneath a moon,
bright and full, the
singing cicadas suddenly
hushed. A herd
of elephants
moved by.

Not far away, an impala lay with ears alert. He glanced up, alarmed. *There was a rustle nearby!*

Then he breathed again. It was only a thirsty old tortoise stumbling past on its way to the waterhole.

Beside the water, still as glass, hatchling turtles struggled from a nest. Blinking at the stars, they scrambled for the safety of the pool, while on the bank the crocodiles slept.

Wild dogs ran by, as dawn broke, and finally the thirsty old tortoise caught sight of the water.

She wanted a drink, but the bank in her way was steep. She teetered forward . . .

Over she tumbled and rolled, then toppled to a halt on her back.

The earth shuddered.
The elephants were coming. She could feel it in the ground!

Terrified, the tortoise retreated into her shell as mighty elephants squashed and crushed all around her.

Then a great foot rose up and came down on top of her . . .

. . . and carefully rolled her over onto her feet.
An idle crocodile watched as the elephants – and the
tortoise – drank . . .

. . . and nearby, trampled and weak, one last baby turtle struggled from the nest. Too late, the darkness had passed. He would have to take his chances in daylight.

A large crocodile noticed his tiny movements.

Fascinated, the crocodile hoisted itself up and came for a closer look.

Sensing danger, the turtle hurried for the water . . .

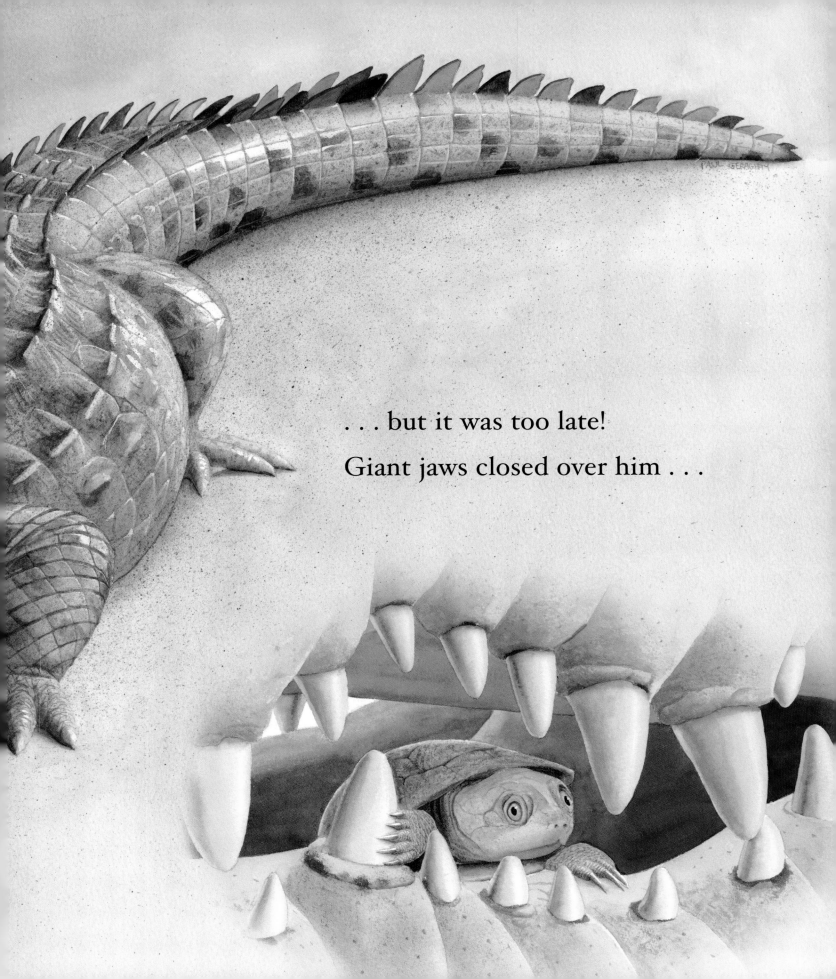

. . . but it was too late!

Giant jaws closed over him . . .

. . . and very gently the great crocodile carried her captive down to the water.

There she floated into the cool, opened her mouth and set the baby free.

But the peace was soon broken by a commotion on the bank.

The wild dogs had found the impala!

He ran for his life. He ran till his throat burned, but the dogs were getting nearer. He could almost feel their hot breath on his haunches . . .

In a last, desperate bid for freedom, he plunged into the pool and began to swim.

Too tired to think, he ploughed onwards. He was now more worried about drowning, than the dogs that waited for him to come back to land.

Exhausted, he flailed for the shallows, and finally stood shivering, as the dogs splashed into the water to get him . . .

Just then, a great shape rose up between them.
A hippopotamus stood threatening the dogs! He kept
the pack of hunters at bay.

Then, turning to the timid impala, he opened his mouth to protect and revive him.

Among the reeds, a tiny turtle watched. So did a drinking tortoise. They watched as the hippopotamus stood with its jaws around the impala, to help it get warm and strong again.

And so ended a wonderful day at the waterhole.